Finally, when Mama was fully satisfied with how the food was arranged and all six places were set out, the Bear family and their friends sat down to their picnic lunch. There were "yums" all around as the picnickers attacked those delicious picnic goodies. "Yums" for the trout, "yums" for the honeycomb, "yums" for the potato salad, and "yums" for the pickles. But they never got to "yums" for the chocolate cake or the cherry pie, because those "yums" suddenly turned into bloodcurdling "yows," "yipes," and "yips" as one after the other, the members of the picnic were bitten on their backsides.

BIG CHAPTER BOOKS

The Berenstain Bears and the Drug Free Zone
The Berenstain Bears and the New Girl in Town
The Berenstain Bears Gotta Dance!
The Berenstain Bears and the Nerdy Nephew
The Berenstain Bears Accept No Substitutes
The Berenstain Bears and the Female Fullback
The Berenstain Bears and the Red-Handed Thief
The Berenstain Bears and the Wheelchair Commando
The Berenstain Bears and the School Scandal Sheet
The Berenstain Bears and the Galloping Ghost
The Berenstain Bears at Camp Crush
The Berenstain Bears and the Giddy Grandma
The Berenstain Bears and the Dress Code
The Berenstain Bears' Media Madness
The Berenstain Bears in the Freaky Funhouse
The Berenstain Bears and the Showdown at Chainsaw Gap
The Berenstain Bears in Maniac Mansion
The Berenstain Bears at the Teen Rock Cafe
The Berenstain Bears and the Bermuda Triangle
The Berenstain Bears and the Ghost of the Auto Graveyard
The Berenstain Bears and the Haunted Hayride
The Berenstain Bears and Queenie's Crazy Crush
The Berenstain Bears and the Big Date
The Berenstain Bears and the Love Match
The Berenstain Bears and the Perfect Crime (Almost)
The Berenstain Bears Go Platinum
The Berenstain Bears and the G-Rex Bones
The Berenstain Bears Lost in Cyberspace
The Berenstain Bears in the Wax Museum
The Berenstain Bears Go Hollywood
The Berenstain Bears and No Guns Allowed
The Berenstain Bears and the Great Ant Attack

The Berenstain Bears and the GREAT ANT ATTACK

by the Berenstains

A BIG CHAPTER BOOK™

Random House New York

Contents

1. The Balance of Nature 1

2. One of Our Ants Is Missing 10

3. Great Day for a Picnic 13

4. Early Warning 24

5. A Short Course in Ant Science 33

6. To the Tower! 43

7. Never Fear!
   Dr. Smythe-Jones Is Here! 49

8. Emergency Powers 59

9. Two Close Calls 69

10. A Closer Look 80

11. Countdown! 87

12. Help for the Bens 96

Chapter One

The Balance of Nature

"How about if we go to a movie tonight? There's a terrific film playing at the Beartown multiplex," said Brother Bear one evening as the Bear family was having supper.

"We might just do that," said Papa. "What's this terrific film called?"

"It's called *Giant Insects from Outer Space,*" said Brother.

"Well, you can count me out," said Sister, who had a problem with insects.

"That's okay," said Brother. "You can take in another film. They always have a G-rated film for scaredy-bears."

"All right, then, Mr. Smart-face. You can count me *in!*" said Sister.

So the Bear family cleaned up the supper things and went to see *Giant Insects from Outer Space.* It was about these giant insects who came in spaceships to attack Earth. They were as big as school buses and looked like a cross between a cockroach and an ant, with a little rhinoceros beetle thrown in.

It was a very scary movie!

Sister was proud of getting through it (she did so by covering her eyes during the

scariest parts). And she was proud of getting through the night without having a
movie nightmare.

But just outside of town, not more than a
mile away from the Bear family's tree
house, a certain professor and his genius
nephew were in their laboratory working on
a secret experiment that just might turn
into a real living nightmare.

The next afternoon, the Bear family was sitting around the tree house living room relaxing. Brother was playing a hand-held monster game. Papa was reading the newspaper. Mama was looking through a garden magazine. And Sister was thinking about *Giant Insects from Outer Space*. As she sat there thinking about one of the scarier parts, a small spider let itself down on a strand of silk right in front of her face.

"YIPE!" screamed Sister, sending the frightened spider scurrying back up the strand of silk.

YIPE!

"My goodness," said Papa. "There's no need to be afraid of spiders. Spiders have more reason to be afraid of you than you have to be afraid of them."

"I'm not afraid of them," said Sister. "I just don't like them."

Papa went back to reading his newspaper and Sister went back to thinking about *Giant Insects from Outer Space*. After thinking awhile, she said, "Papa?"

"Yes, dear," said Papa.

"Why do there have to be insects?"

"I'm not sure I understand your question, my dear," said Papa.

"Well, I just mean why do there have to be insects? They're so buggy and icky. I mean like creepy spiders and itchy mosquitoes and those nasty green flies that bite. I mean, what good are they? Why do we have to have them?"

"That's a very interesting question," said Papa. "And I suppose the best answer is that they're all part of nature's great scheme. All those icky, buggy creatures, all creatures and plants, in fact, and even the Earth itself, make up what's called the balance of nature."

"That's right," said Brother. "That's what Teacher Bob says. We learned about that in biology. He says that if the bees and the butterflies didn't carry pollen from plant to plant, we wouldn't have fruits and vegetables."

"Or flowers," said Mama, looking up from her gardening magazine. "And I might add,

if there were no mosquitoes, dragonflies, and water bugs for the trout to eat, we wouldn't be having honey-cured trout for supper tonight."

"Yum!" said Brother.

"Thank goodness for the balance of nature," said Papa. Which was all very well, but Sister still had a problem with insects.

Sister Bear wasn't the only one who had a problem with insects. Farmer Ben, whose farm was just down the road from the Bear family's tree house, had a big problem with insects. Especially with the ones that ate his crops. The mere mention of the corn borer, the wheat worm, or the barley moth sent

Farmer Ben into a fury. While Farmer Ben had a good heart, he also had a terrible temper. Just the mention of those insects made him wave his arms, jump up and down, and say words that burnt the very air.

If the Bear family had looked out a window that afternoon, they would have seen Farmer Ben doing just that. He was with Crop Duster Joe. They were at the place where Ben's corn, wheat, and barley fields met. Joe had the same argument with Ben every year. He was waiting for Ben to calm down so he could tell him the same thing he had told him the year before and the year before that. "I can't use anything

stronger, Ben. It's against the law. I can only dust with approved chemicals, and DDT isn't approved. Try to understand. All the environmental folks are trying to do is preserve the balance of nature. And besides, if I used DDT, I could lose my license."

"Well, dang your license! Dang the balance of nature!"

Mrs. Ben, the only one who could calm Ben down when he was in a temper, had heard the ruckus all the way from the farmhouse. "Now, come on, Ben. It doesn't do any good to rant and rave. Come on back to the house. I've got some warm milk with a dash of strawberry honey waiting for you. And, Joe..."

"Yes, ma'am?"

"You just dust the crops the same as you did last year."

"Yes, ma'am."

Chapter Two
One of Our Ants Is Missing

Meanwhile, that certain professor (it was Professor Actual Factual) and his genius nephew (it was Ferdy Factual) had just discovered that one of their ants was missing. Normally, a missing ant wouldn't be of great concern. But this was no ordinary ant. It was a super-ant. At least that's what the professor and his nephew were calling the new species they had developed in their laboratory at the Bearsonian Institution.

"Look, Uncle!" said Ferdy. "That superant has eaten its way right through the ant-proof cage!"

"Why, bless my spectacles! So it has! Tell me, Nephew," said the professor, "was it one of our winged specimens?"

"Yes, Uncle," said Ferdy, "I'm afraid it was. Could that be a problem?"

"Hmm," said the professor. "Well, it's worth thinking about. The fact that it was winged means we are looking at two possibilities. Possibility one: it was a male. In which case, no harm done. It will forage briefly, then expire. Possibility two—and this is a little more worrisome—it was a queen. But while she may lay eggs and even have a few hatch out, no real harm will be done, because without the support of a colony, she and her offspring will soon die."

Now, Ferdy was no more a mind reader than you and I, but he saw a cloud of concern pass over his uncle's face and knew that another possibility had just occurred to him. "What is it, Uncle?" he asked. "Is there a possibility three?"

"Yes," said Actual Factual with a nervous chuckle. "But it's so far-fetched that I refuse even to discuss it."

"If you say so, Unc," said Ferdy. "But don't you think we should check ant security? We wouldn't want any more to escape."

"Good thinking. Good thinking."

Chapter Three

Great Day for a Picnic

The balance of nature looked fine and dandy a couple of days later when the Bear family decided to go on a picnic. The grass was still green, the bees were still buzzing, the woodpeckers were still pecking, and all was right with the world. Or at least so it seemed to the Bear family as they headed for their favorite picnic spot, the beautiful meadow just south of Bear Country's most important museum: the Bearsonian Institution.

Brother and Sister had brought friends along. They were Cousin Fred, who was a cousin as well as a friend, and Babs Bruno, who happened to be the daughter of Beartown's chief of police. The cubs got to the meadow ahead of Mama and Papa, who were carrying big baskets of picnic goodies, so they got to choose the picnic spot. It was such a hot day that they chose a spot beside a big rock so they would have some shade as the day wore on.

"Is this spot okay?" asked Sister as Papa unfolded the big red-and-white-checked tablecloth they always used for picnics.

"Just fine," said Papa as he shook out the

tablecloth and settled it down on the grass.
"What a great day for a picnic!" he said.
"Just look at that beautiful blue sky. Just
breathe in that air."

"We're hungry! When do we eat?" cried
Brother and Sister, jumping up and down.
Cousin Fred and Babs Bruno were hungry,
too. But they were too polite to shout and
jump up and down.

"Now, just calm down. We'll eat when I
say so," said Mama. "I want to rest up a bit
after that long walk."

"Good thinking, Mama," said Papa. "You sit in the shade while the cubs and I put out the spread."

And what a spread it was! There was honey-cured trout, French-fried honeycomb, home-baked bread, lettuce and tomatoes from Mama's garden, potato salad with pine nuts, two thermoses of cold milk, a big jar of Papa's favorite homemade pickles, and for dessert, chocolate cake and cherry pie! And there were plenty of sturdy paper picnic things to serve it on and eat with.

"No sneaking tastes, please," said Papa when he saw Brother getting ready to scoop up a finger-load of icing from the chocolate cake. Brother returned the favor a little later when he caught Papa green-handed sneaking a crunchy bite of pickle.

"I can't put it back in the jar," said Papa

> I ALREADY BIT IT.

with a guilty grin, "because I already bit it."

"Just put what's left of it on your plate, my dear," said Mama, "until we all sit down to our picnic lunch."

Finally, when Mama was fully satisfied with how the food was arranged and all six places were set out, the Bear family and their friends sat down to their picnic lunch. There were "yums" all around as the picnickers attacked those delicious picnic goodies. "Yums" for the trout, "yums" for the honeycomb, "yums" for the potato

salad, and "yums" for the pickles. But they never got to "yums" for the chocolate cake or the cherry pie, because those "yums" suddenly turned into bloodcurdling "yows," "yipes," and "yips" as one after the other, the members of the picnic were bitten on their backsides.

"Ants!" screamed the picnickers as they leaped up in pain. But they weren't just ants. They were super-ants, and those super-ants were eating their lunch, paper plates and all.

"Look at them," cried Papa. "They're huge!"

The picnickers danced away from the picnic spread so as not to get bitten on their feet.

"Those aren't ordinary ants," said Cousin Fred. "I think we'd better try to catch one. It may be some strange new kind of ant."

"I don't know if that's safe," said Brother. "Look at what they're doing to our lunch!" The chocolate cake and the cherry pie were disappearing before their eyes. "Look! One of them just went into the pickle jar. I think I can catch it!" said Brother, who was very fast on his feet—his soccer moves were famous. He leaped in, capped the jar, and leaped out.

"There's one on your foot!" cried Sister. She knocked it off before it could bite. The group stared at the captured ant. Not only was it large and powerful-looking, it had huge jaws. There had been one pickle left in the jar, and the ant had already eaten

halfway through it. They could hear the crunching right through the glass jar.

"Look!" cried Papa, pointing across the meadow. "There's a whole army of 'em headed this way. Quick! Up on the rock!"

Papa helped the cubs and Mama up onto the big rock, then climbed up after them. The army of ants was a frightening sight. It looked like a fast-moving ribbon of black velvet flowing over the ground. The bears huddled together on the big rock. They watched in amazement as the great ribbon of ants ate their entire picnic, divided, went around the rock, rejoined, and continued on its destructive way.

"It's like that giant insect movie," said Sister.

"It's much worse," said Brother. "Because this isn't a movie!"

"Oh, dear!" said Mama. "They've eaten

my red-and-white-checked tablecloth!"

"Hmm," said Papa. "The only things they haven't eaten are those two thermoses."

"What's that funny smell?" asked Babs Bruno, sniffing the air. "Hey, it smells like...grape juice!"

"How weird," said Papa. "It does smell like grape juice. How's our pickle jar ant doing?"

"It's finished the pickle," said Fred. "Now it's running around looking for more."

"I think it's safe to get down off this rock now. You know something?" said Papa as he helped Mama down. "I think Cousin Fred is onto something. I think it may be some new kind of ant. We're going to have to show this fellow to an expert—and it's a lucky coincidence that our good friend Professor Actual Factual is available just across the meadow at the Bearsonian Institution."

Chapter Four

Early Warning

Of course, it wasn't a coincidence at all.

When the professor saw the ant in the pickle jar and heard about the great army of ants that ate just about everything in sight and smelled like grape juice, he fell into a chair as if the weight of the world had just dropped on him. Ferdy looked pretty worried, too.

"What's going on, Professor?" asked Papa. "What's happening out there?"

"I'm very much afraid," said the professor, "that possibility three is happening."

"Possibility three? What's possibility three?" asked Papa.

"Possibility three," said the professor in a low, trembling voice, "is a disaster of such epic proportions that it boggles the mind."

"Somebody get the professor a glass of water," said Mama. "He looks a little sick."

"I *am* sick, dear lady—sick with guilt over the awful thing I have done. Oh, sorrow! Oh, grief! The work of a lifetime brought to naught because of the escape of a single ant."

"I don't mean to argue with you, Professor," said Papa. "But it's not a single ant. It's thousands of ants. Thousands and thousands of 'em chewing their way across Bear

Country, devouring everything in their path. I saw 'em with my own eyes. I felt 'em with my own backside!"

But the professor just moaned and groaned some more. "What have I done? What have I done?"

"Please, Uncle," said Ferdy. "Moaning and groaning isn't going to help. You've got to get ahold of yourself. I think I may have figured out what you meant by 'possibility three,' and you're right. We may be looking at a very serious situation. We know there's at least one colony out there. But there could be more. Remember, this super-ant we've developed is a hybrid. We have no idea how fast it reproduces."

The professor squared his shoulders. "Sorry about my moment of weakness, friends," he said. "But Ferdy is right. For the sake of our survival, we must assume

IT DOESN'T FEEL SO FORTUNATE.

the worst. First, let me thank you. It's most fortunate that you brought us early warning of your encounter with the super-ant colony."

"It doesn't feel so fortunate," said Papa, rubbing his backside.

"As Ferdy suggested, the nature of hybrids is very unpredictable. You have brought us one very important piece of information about the super-ant: its eating habits."

"Its habits are very simple, Professor,"

said Papa. "It just eats everything in sight."

"It's not quite that simple," said the professor. "Let me ask you a couple of questions. First, you say that your group climbed up on a big rock for safety. Is that correct?"

"Yes," said Papa.

"And the ants made no attempt to climb the rock to get at you?"

"That's right," said Brother.

"Next, you say the ants ate everything except two thermoses? Is that correct?"

"That's right," said Mama.

"What were they made of?"

"I believe they were made of aluminum," said Papa.

"So what?" asked Sister. "What difference does it make?"

"It makes a great deal of difference, I'm afraid," said Actual Factual. "It means that this new kind of ant that my nephew and I

28

have developed is pretty close to being an omnivore. That is, it can eat and digest organic material—*all* organic material!"

"What the heck is organic material?" asked Brother.

"It's everything that's alive or has ever been alive," said the professor.

"But that's just about *everything!*" said Babs.

"I'm afraid so," said the professor. "Everything except rocks, metals, and other earth substances." Professor Actual Factual was not only director of the Bearsonian Institution but also one of Bear Country's

BUT THAT'S JUST ABOUT <u>EVERYTHING!</u>

greatest scientists. It took a lot to frighten him. But there was no question about it— the professor looked very frightened. When the bears realized what he meant about the super-ants' eating habits, they got pretty frightened themselves. The questions came thick and fast.

"Does that mean they can eat *us*?"

"What's a hybrid?"

"What's going to happen?"

"What's possibility three?"

"Why do they smell like grape juice?"

"What are we going to do?"

Fear was spreading throughout the room.

"Well," said Professor Actual Factual, "the first thing I'm going to do is call Dr. Minerva Smythe-Jones at the university. Dr. Smythe-Jones is the world's leading authority on Hymenoptera."

"Hymen-*who*-tera?" asked Sister.

"That's the scientific name for the animal order that ants are part of. Minerva, who is an old friend of mine—we went to university together—is just about the only one in the country who might know how to stop them. If, indeed, they need to be stopped. After all, we do not yet know the size of the problem. If there's just one colony out there, the problem should be manageable. If, on the other hand, this hybrid turns out to have strong reproductive powers...Well, I'd better place my call to Dr. Smythe-

Jones." As the professor went to place the call, the questions started again.

"What are hybrids?"

"Can anything stop them?"

Ferdy raised his hand to stop the flow of questions. "My friends, instead of answering your questions one by one, I think it would be better to give you a short course in ant science. Please follow me into the laboratory."

Chapter Five

A Short Course in Ant Science

The laboratory was a long room with shelves on either side. On the shelves were large glassed-in ant colonies.

"Now, these," said Ferdy, pointing to one of the colonies, "are ordinary Bear Country

ants. Like all ants, they live in colonies, which are groups that range in size from thousands to millions. And as with most ants, this type lives underground. As you can see, they have dug out a network of chambers connected by tunnels. Our glass cases enable us to make cross-sections of our ant colonies, so that we can see right into some of the chambers and tunnels and observe the ants."

"What are they doing in this chamber?" asked Fred, pointing to the largest one.

"That's the queen's chamber," said Ferdy. "It's the most important chamber in the entire colony. That's because it's where this one very large ant, the queen, lays the eggs from which new members of the colony will hatch. You can see that some of her eggs have already hatched and have turned into caterpillar-like forms called larvae. Only the

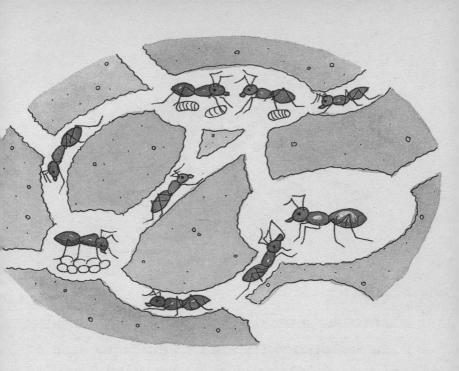

queen produces eggs. The smaller ants around her are females called workers. They bring her food."

"Hey," said Brother, "one of the workers is stealing a larva!"

Ferdy chuckled. "Not stealing, Brother," he said. "She is taking it to the brooding chamber, where workers care for the larvae. Eventually, the larvae spin protective

cocoons around themselves, and inside these cocoons they turn into pupae—or a 'pupa' for just one. The pupae will become full-grown ants. Now watch. There she goes, carrying the egg through a tunnel…to the brooding chamber."

"What does the queen do when she's finished laying eggs?" asked Brother.

"Lays more eggs," said Ferdy. "That's all she does: lays eggs until she dies. Most of her babies will become workers in the colony. Workers can't fly. But a few of the female babies are born with wings. These are future queens, who will fly away and establish new colonies elsewhere."

While Ferdy's short course in ant science was very interesting, it was also a little scary. Papa swallowed hard when he realized that queens flying away and starting new colonies was exactly what Professor Actual Factual was worried about.

Babs pointed at a winged ant she'd spotted. "Is that one of the future queens?"

"No," said Ferdy. "That's a male."

"Where's the king's chamber?" asked Sister.

"There is no king's chamber," said Ferdy, "because there is no king. All the males are winged. They fly off after future queens and mate with them."

"What else do they do?" asked Brother.

"Nothing at all," said Ferdy.

"Sounds like a pretty easy life," said Brother.

"But a short one," Ferdy pointed out. "The males live only a fraction of the time the females do."

Ferdy led the cubs to the neighboring case. "Now, this colony," he said, "consists of an entirely different species of ant, one that is definitely not from Bear Country."

"Where is it from?" asked Brother.

"The jungles of Bearneo," said Ferdy. "Notice that they are twice the size of the Bear Country ants. And see how they move through the tunnels?"

"They're faster than the Bear Country ants," observed Fred.

"Yes," said Ferdy. "In the wild, they chase down and eat beetles and other large insects—even toads, lizards, and salamanders. From time to time, an entire colony will move a great distance and establish a new home, capturing food along the way. During a move, the large queen is actually carried by worker ants. It's quite a sight. A colony on the move looks like a great army. And that's why they are called army ants."

"Do the Bear Country ants eat animals, too?" asked Brother.

"Only occasionally," said Ferdy. "Mostly they eat plants—seeds, grain, tender shoots, and leaves. That's the problem with them. They wreak havoc on crops. Just ask Farmer

Ben. Our goal in mating our local ants with these jungle ants was to develop a hybrid that would eat wheat worms, corn borers, and barley moths instead of wheat, corn, and barley."

"You seem to have overshot your goal," said Babs.

"Disastrously so," said Ferdy.

"You said those ants that attacked our picnic were hybrids. What's a hybrid?" asked Brother.

"Most species," explained Ferdy, "do not mate with different species. And even if they do, they rarely produce young. But occasionally, it does happen. That's a hybrid. That's what happened with our Bear Country ants and our army ants. Come and look at this third colony."

The cubs' eyes widened as they approached the third case. "Hey!" said

Brother. "Those are the ants that attacked us!"

"That's the problem," said Ferdy. "The ant that escaped must have been a queen, because she produced a colony in just a few days. I think that's the possibility three the professor's worried about. It sounds far-fetched, but I think our escaped queen must have been adopted by some local ants that lost their queen. It's just about the only possibility I can think of that explains the colony that you ran into."

"Scary," said Brother.

"Very scary," agreed Ferdy.

"What do you call this hybrid?" asked Fred.

"It's brand-new, so we had to name it ourselves," said Ferdy. "We're calling it *Antus*

maximus—in English, 'super-ant.' I selected this name because, in our hybrid species, the traits and habits of the two parent species did not just blend, as they usually do, but were also greatly magnified."

Ferdy's short course in the science of ants sort of trailed off. He looked worried. "I wish we knew what was happening out there," he said. "Is that one colony going to be the end of it, or will there be more?"

"What about the observation tower?" asked Brother. "Why don't we go up there and look?"

"Brilliant idea, Brother!" cried Ferdy. "Follow me!"

"You cubs go ahead," said Papa. "The professor is having a little difficulty getting through to the ant expert. I think he needs a little extra support right now. Mama and I will stay with him."

Chapter Six

To the Tower!

The cubs raced up the circular stair that led to the top of the observation tower. The tower was one of the main parts of the Bearsonian Institution. Astronomy was one of the professor's special interests, so the tower had a large Star Gazer telescope for exploring the galaxy. But it also had a pair of powerful field glasses. Ferdy immediately grabbed them and began scanning the area.

"Wow!" said Sister. "You can see for miles around up here!"

"There's the colony that attacked your picnic," said Ferdy. "And, oh, my goodness!

I see another colony! And another! Good grief! There are now three colonies. That's bad enough. But there's something even scarier going on out there. Something that goes against everything I know about ant science."

"What's that, Ferdy?" asked Brother.

"Well," said Ferdy, still peering through the glasses, "instead of fighting—ant colonies are always at war with each other—they seem to be cooperating, moving along beside each other. Here, take a look." Ferdy handed the field glasses to Brother.

"Yeah," said Brother. "I see what you mean."

"I don't like the sound of that," said Babs. She took something out of her pocket and

and began punching buttons.

"What are you doing?" asked Sister.

"Calling my father on my cell phone. This ant thing looks like a real emergency. It's a matter for the police...Hello, hello. This is Babs Bruno. I have to talk to the chief...Well, tell him to call my cell phone number. It's an emergency."

"Let me see!" demanded Sister. Brother gave her a turn at the field glasses. "Hey, I see what you mean. It looks like they're making friends."

Babs's cell phone rang.

"Yes, Dad, it's me! I'm over in the Bearsonian tower, and something awful is happening. There's this weird army of ants! There're zillions of 'em!...You know about it? Okay! Okay! See you!...

"My dad knows all about it. He's calling from the police helicopter. He helped the

47

professor get through to that Dr. Smythe-Jones. He's picked her up and they're headed this way."

"Here they come!" cried Sister as the *chop-chop-chop* of the helicopter got louder and louder.

"Look!" cried Fred. "They're going to land right in front of the museum!"

"Back down to the lab!" shouted Ferdy. They tore down the circular stairs and rushed to the lab.

Chapter Seven
Never Fear!
Dr. Smythe-Jones Is Here!

The chief and Dr. Smythe-Jones had already arrived by the time the cubs got back to the laboratory. Dr. Smythe-Jones was a large, forceful person.

"My dear old friend," she cried, enfolding the professor in a big, smothering hug. "So grand to see you again after all these years!"

"Good to see you again, Minerva," choked the professor. Dr. Smythe-Jones introduced herself all around.

"Old friend," she said to the professor, "the chief here tells me you've got yourself a little hymenoptery problem. Why don't you tell me about it?" She took notes as Professor Actual Factual told of the events that had led up to the present situation: the development of *Antus maximus,* the escape of a queen, the growth of a colony, and the attack on the picnickers. He also pointed out that the super-ants could eat all organic materials.

"Uncle, I'm afraid there are further developments," said Ferdy.

Dr. Smythe-Jones took notes furiously as Ferdy told of their observations from the tower. "Two additional colonies, ya say? That makes three. But please tell me again about this strange behavior you observed."

"Well, Uncle and I are not hymenopterists like you, Doctor. But I've always understood that ant colonies don't get along. That they are usually at war with each other."

"That's right," she said. "Just what did you see that makes you think otherwise?"

"Well, these three colonies weren't going at each other as if they were about to fight.

They were just moving along, sidling up to each other. It was almost as if they were communicating."

"Hmm," said Dr. Smythe-Jones. "Communicating, ya say. Hmm." She stood up. "All right, Actual. Let me have a look at this super-ant of yours." She followed the professor over to one of the glassed-in super-ant colonies and looked in. "Well, now," said the ant expert as she looked at the hybrid ants that the professor and Ferdy had developed. "I've seen just about every type of ant known to science. But I've never seen an ant that looked like this big fellow—almost twice as big as these jungle ants. I can see why you're calling it *Antus maximus*. Look at those jaws. Look at that thorax. Somebody give me a magnifying glass." Ferdy handed her one. She selected one of the super-ants and stared at it long

and hard through the magnifying glass.
Then she put down the glass and turned to
Actual Factual.

"My compliments, Professor," she said.
"You and this bright little nephew of yours
have made a great contribution to the noble
science of hymenoptery. *Antus maximus* is
the finest-looking ant I have ever seen."

"Well," said the professor, "Ferdy and I
thank you for those kind words. But, Minerva, the reason we have brought you here
is—" The sound of a siren interrupted him.

"That'll be Officer Marguerite," said the

chief. "I radioed her in the police car from the chopper." There were hurried hellos all around as Officer Marguerite came into the laboratory.

"You see any ants on your way over?" asked the chief.

"Just a couple of flying ones," said Marguerite.

"Oh, dear!" said the professor. "They could be queens flying off to start new colonies."

"Or," said Dr. Smythe-Jones, "they could be males just scouting around."

"We don't mean to be a nuisance, Chief," said Mama. "But what you said about their eating habits, Professor, worries me. Those super-ants could eat us right out of tree house and home. Could Marguerite take us back home? Just as a precaution? We'd like to pick up our photo albums and a few other family bearlooms just in case."

"Do it, Marguerite," said the chief. "But the cubs had better stay here at the Bearsonian. It's solid stone."

"Can't you stay here, Mama?" asked Sister.

"Don't worry, my dear," said Mama. "Papa and I will be safe in the police car with Officer Marguerite."

But Sister worried as she listened to the eerie sound of the police siren trail off in the distance as Marguerite raced for the endangered tree house.

Dr. Smythe-Jones turned to Ferdy. "Young fellow, to complete my report, I need to know more about the strange, friendly behavior of super-ant colonies. But I'd like to see it for myself."

"Follow me, Doctor!" cried Ferdy. Professor Actual Factual, Dr. Smythe-Jones, Chief Bruno, and the cubs fell in behind Ferdy as he led the way to the top of the tower. Dr. Smythe-Jones seized the field glasses.

"Amazing!" she said as she scanned the

horizon. It was as though she was watching the greatest show on earth. Finally, she put the glasses down and fell heavily into a chair. "Remarkable," she said. "I wouldn't have believed it if I hadn't seen it with my own eyes. You'd better have a look, Professor."

"Good grief!" said the professor. "Ferdy was right. Not only are they communicating, the three colonies are forming an army the likes of which the world has never seen!"

"The glasses, please," said Chief Bruno... "Gad! What a sight! They look like a dark shadow moving over the earth, leaving everything brown and dead in its path. And look! They're heading for Farmer Ben's farm! Quick, Babs! Give me your cell phone!"

"Who are you calling?" asked Babs as her father pushed furiously at the buttons.

"The mayor," said the chief. "He's got to declare an emergency!"

Chapter Eight

Emergency Powers

Mayor Horace J. Honeypot was sitting behind his important-looking desk in his important-looking office thinking how wonderful it was to have such an important job. He had been reelected more times than anybody could count. He wasn't a bad mayor, but neither was he an especially good one. The biggest complaint against him was that he kept putting things off. He just didn't seem to be able to make decisions. But somehow he kept getting reelected. There was a little ditty about why that was so. It went like this:

Why does the mayor always win?
Because half the population's his kin!

The light that signaled an incoming call was flashing on Mayor Honeypot's phone. But the mayor wasn't in the mood for phone calls. The trouble with phone calls was that the callers usually needed some sort of a decision. Besides, his secretary in the outer office would answer it. That's what secretaries were for.

But Mayor Honeypot's peace and quiet were shattered when his secretary burst in and shouted, "Pick up line two, Mr. Mayor!

It's Chief Bruno! He says it's an emergency!"

"Oh, dear," said the mayor. He certainly wasn't in the mood for emergencies. Reluctantly, he picked up line two. As soon as the phone was off the hook, the chief's voice split the air.

The mayor had another problem with emergencies. Whenever he got excited, he tended to get the fronts and backs of his words mixed up. "Would you please shop stouting, Chief—er, would you please stop shouting? And would you sleak more spowly—er, speak more slowly?…But, Chief, I can't declare an emergency because of a few ants!"

But, of course, it was more than a few ants. It was a whole army of ants. And armies have scouts. And one of them scouted its way into the seat of the mayor's

pants and took a big bite out of him!

The mayor's scream of pain echoed through City Hall. He leaped so high that you might have thought gravity had been overcome. In fact, those super-ants were helping folks overcome gravity all over town.

"Yipe!" shouted Judge Gavel across the street in the courthouse.

"Yipe!" screamed Miss Goodbear, the Beartown librarian, just down the way.

"Yowl!" yelled Mr. Vault, president of the Beartown Bank and Trust, one block over.

As soon as the mayor got over his painful ant bite, he declared an emergency. He had his secretary call the radio and television stations and the newspapers and tell them about it.

Meanwhile, back at the Bearsonian, Professor Actual Factual, Chief Bruno, Ferdy, and the other cubs were waiting for Dr. Smythe-Jones to finish her notes.

"Well, that does it," she said after dotting a final "i" and crossing a last "t." She stood and looked Professor Actual Factual in the eye. "Professor," she said, "I've always known what a great scientist you are. Your achievements in such varied fields of study as the environment, astronomy, and atomic science are known far and wide. But what you, a non-specialist, and your nephew have done in the field of hymenoptery is truly astonishing. I would go so far as to say that your development of *Antus maximus* will go down as the greatest achievement in the history of ant science. I bow to you, my old friend. The name Actual Factual will live forever in the annals of science."

"As I said before, Doctor," said the professor, "we really do thank you for those

kind words. But quite aside from that, what do you propose we do about the superants?"

"Do?" said Dr. Smythe-Jones in a puzzled tone of voice. "Well, I don't know what *you're* going to do about them. But what *I'm* going to do is go back to the university, write up my report on your glorious achievement, and send it off to *Ant: The Journal of Hymenoptery*. Now, Chief, if I could trouble you for a lift in your helicopter—"

"But you can't be serious, Doctor!" protested Professor Actual Factual.

"I beg your pardon, Professor," said Dr. Smythe-Jones. "I've never been *more* serious in my life. Now, Chief, as I was saying—"

"But don't you understand?" said Actual Factual. "The super-ants must be stopped! If they are not, they will eat all plant life, all food. They will make the Earth uninhabitable."

"I beg to differ," said the ant scientist. "It will be perfectly inhabitable—by ants. Look at it this way: Ants were here millions of years before we were, and they will be here millions of years after we're gone. Now, Chief—"

"But please, Minerva! I implore you! You're the only one who might know how to stop them. Please! What about the future?"

"What about it? There'll be a future whatever we do. If you please, Chief—"

"But, Minerva! What about your family?" cried the professor.

"My family?" said Dr. Smythe-Jones. "Ants are the most magnificent creatures ever designed by nature. *They* are my family. Again, it's been nice meeting you all—"

"Dr. Smythe-Jones?" said Brother.

"Yes?"

"What about us?" asked Brother. "What about *our* future?" Brother's question seemed to soften Dr. Smythe-Jones just a little.

"And what about the future of science?" asked Ferdy. "What about the search for knowledge?"

WHAT ABOUT US?

"What about the balance of nature?" asked Sister. "What about that?"

Maybe it was Sister's question that changed Dr. Smythe-Jones's mind, or maybe it was her little-girl voice. But whatever it was, the great ant scientist agreed to help with the fight against *Antus maximus*.

"Listen closely," Dr. Smythe-Jones said. "Especially you, Chief. Because if we're going to stop the super-ants, we're going to have to move fast."

"I can do that," said the chief. "The mayor has given me emergency powers."

"The only thing that can stop them now is an insecticide called Super DDT. It's very dangerous, but the university has kept some on hand to experiment with. Now, here's what I suggest..."

Chapter Nine

Two Close Calls

"Faster! Faster! We're almost there!" cried Papa as the Bear family's tree house came in view.

"No sign of the ants yet," said Mama as Officer Marguerite pushed the police car to its limits.

"I'm worried about the cubs," said Mama. "I wonder if we did the right thing leaving them at the Bearsonian."

"Of course we did," said Papa. "The

Bearsonian's made of stone. That's one thing those super-ants can't eat."

"Oh, dear," said Mama. "I'm beginning to smell grape juice again."

"That means they're getting close," said Papa. "Look! Over there! I see them. There're millions of 'em! They're all over Farmer Ben's farm. Wait! They're after Farmer Ben. He and his missus are trying

to escape on their tractor. We have to rescue them!"

"Hang on!" cried Officer Marguerite as she turned and headed right for the on-coming horde of ants. "Prepare for a sickening crunch! We're going to have to drive right through them!"

"Into the car! Into the car!" shouted Papa

as Farmer and Mrs. Ben clambered down from the tractor.

"Phew!" said Farmer Ben. "That was a close call!"

Which, indeed, it was. While the super-ants couldn't eat the tractor, which was made of steel, they were eating through the huge tractor tires as if they were cheese.

Crop Duster Joe was sitting in his office way over on the other side of town, working on his schedule. Just outside of his office on a small airstrip was his airplane, an old two-wing Jenny that was perfect for crop-dusting. Joe was half-listening to music on his radio as he worked on his schedule. But his ears perked up when somebody broke in on the music.

"This is an emergency," said the radio announcer. "We are breaking in on our regular program to bring you Mayor Horace J.

Honeypot, speaking from City Hall."

"My cellow fitizens—er, my fellow citizens...YIPE! YOWL! YIP!"

"Since we seem to have lost our signal from City Hall, I will read what the mayor was about to say: 'My fellow citizens, our fair city is being attacked by ants—I repeat,

our fair city is being attacked by ants. But these are not ordinary ants...' "

As Joe turned to listen, he caught sight of a large ant out of the corner of his eye. Since Joe was in the crop-dusting business, he knew quite a lot about insects, and he knew it was no ordinary ant. He was about to swat it with his schedule, but when he

BONK!

saw its giant jaws, he decided to go after it with a hammer. *Bonk!* went the hammer. Then he saw another ant, and another, and another. As Joe went after them with his hammer, his phone rang.

"Hello, Crop Duster Joe here...Yes, Chief...I understand...I just killed a few of 'em right here in the office. Uh-huh...Uh-huh...I understand. Let me repeat that, Chief. I'm to fly to the university and pick up a supply of Super DDT. Then I'm to rendezvous with you in the police helicopter over Farmer Ben's farm...Sure, I know where it is. Ben's a regular customer...What's this all about, Chief?...Army ants, you say?...My plane? She's an old Jenny. All wood and fabric, except for the control wires, of course...She's painted with aluminum dope. Why do you ask?" That's when Joe looked out the window and saw a narrow black ribbon of ants going after his plane.

"I'm coming, Jenny! I'm coming!" shouted Joe as he raced the ribbon of ants to the plane. He beat them, but not by much. He hit the ignition. The motor sputtered at first, then coughed into a roar.

"Good old Jenny!" he shouted as the plane took off. But as he pulled back on the stick to climb, he saw that some of the ants had managed to reach the plane. The ones

on the wings seemed to be trying to eat through the aluminum dope. And some were already eating through the bamboo struts that held the biplane together.

The situation was desperate, and desperate situations call for desperate action. He pulled back on the stick and climbed. He climbed to 10,000 feet, which was as high as old Jenny could go. Then he pushed forward on the stick and put her into a steep power dive. Joe's idea was to dive so fast that the slipstream would blow the ants off the plane. Down, down, down roared old Jenny! The question was, which would come off first, the ants or the wings?

As the ground came up to meet him, Joe held his breath and pulled back on the stick to fly up again—and glory be! The wings stayed on and the ants didn't.

Joe thanked his lucky stars and headed for the university.

Chapter Ten

A Closer Look

The chief looked out the front door of the Bearsonian to see if the coast was clear.

"It's hard to be sure, but I don't see any ants. Of course, there could be scouts. But scouts or not, we've got to go ahead with our plan. Okay, I'll make a run for it to the helicopter and get it revved up. Then, when I give you the high sign, you all make a run and climb on."

"Will it hold us all?" asked Brother.

"Easily," said the chief. "It's an old Army surplus chopper. Now be ready for the rotor

wash. It's very powerful. Okay, here I go!"

"There didn't seem to be any scouts," said Dr. Smythe-Jones as the chief climbed into the chopper and started the motor. Within seconds, the rotors were a blur.

"There's the high sign!" cried Ferdy. "Let's go!"

The group, which included the professor, Dr. Smythe-Jones, Ferdy, Brother, Sister, Cousin Fred, and Babs, rushed to the chopper and climbed in.

"Radio central," said the chief. "We're taking off. Do you read me, radio central? Over and out."

"We read you."

Babs, who had been up in her dad's

helicopter many times, showed the group where to sit and how to buckle up.

"How far to this farm?" asked Dr. Smythe-Jones, who was buckled into the co-pilot's seat.

"Not far," said the chief. "You saw it from the tower. We'll be there in a jiffy. I'm going to climb for a better view."

"Gee, I hope Mama and Papa are safe," said Sister.

"Perfectly safe," said the chief. "After

they rescued Ben and his missus, Officer Marguerite took them to the police station. They almost had to tie Ben down. He wanted to go back and beat those ants off with a shovel."

"It's a good thing that he didn't," said Dr. Smythe-Jones. "If he had, there wouldn't have been anything left of him but the shovel."

The chief took the chopper so high they could see for miles around. They could see downtown Beartown, its suburbs, and the surrounding countryside. It was very beautiful, and the idea that this strange breed of ants that the professor and his nephew had developed could destroy it all was on all their minds. Even Dr. Smythe-Jones, who had devoted her life to the study of ants and loved them dearly, knew they had to be stopped.

"There they are!" said the chief. Right at the center of all that beauty was a black spot. It looked almost like an inkblot. It was the army of super-ants. They covered every inch of Farmer Ben's farm. If the super-ants weren't stopped, they would destroy not only Ben's crops but his barn, his silo, and his house as well.

"I wonder what happened to his livestock," said Brother.

"I'm going to take her down for a closer look," said the chief.

"There's that grape juice smell again," said Sister as the chopper went lower. "Doctor Smythe-Jones, may I ask you a question?"

"Of course, my dear," she said.

"Why the heck do those dopey ants smell like grape juice?"

Dr. Smythe-Jones smiled. "All ants smell like grape juice, my dear. It's just that super-ants are bigger, so they have a bigger grape juice smell. The answer is simple. Ants are of the order Hymenoptera. But they are also of the family Formicidae. That's pronounced *for-MIS-uh-dee,* and it means that ant bodies are made mostly of a chemical called formic acid. And grape juice is made of very similar chemicals. That's why ants smell like grape juice."

"That's all very well," said the chief. "But Crop Duster Joe should have been here with the Super DDT by now. I wonder what's keeping him."

Chapter Eleven

Countdown!

What was keeping him was that old Jenny had needed repairs. The ants had not only eaten through some of the struts, they had found some thin places in the aluminum dope on the wings. But Joe had managed some quick repairs and had put the Super DDT into Jenny's dusting tanks. He had made good time getting to the university airport, but was being slowed down by a headwind on the way back. Jenny shuddered and shook as she fought the headwind. "I hope we get there in time," said Joe. "I hope, I hope, I hope."

The group in the helicopter hoped so, too. Farmer Ben's farm was looking worse moment by moment. The chief had brought the chopper down to 1,000 feet. That's where they were supposed to meet Crop Duster Joe's plane. The ants, which had looked like an inkblot from way up high, now looked like a great spreading stain.

"Joe should be here by now," said the chief as they hovered over the ruins of Ben's farm. "We can't hover much longer.

ARE THERE GOOD INSECTS?

We're getting low on gas. Are you sure this Super DDT will stop the super-ants?"

"After what I've seen today, Chief, I'm not sure of anything," said Dr. Smythe-Jones. "The trouble is that Super DDT may be as dangerous as the super-ants."

"Why is that?" asked Cousin Fred.

"The reason we stopped using DDT—and Super DDT's even worse—is that it's bad for the environment. It causes all kinds of problems. It's an excellent insect killer, but it kills good insects as well as bad insects."

"*Are* there good insects?" asked Sister.

"You better believe it," said Dr. Smythe-Jones. "There are honeybees, of course. Certain ants eat aphids that destroy crops. And we'd be in big trouble if we didn't have butterflies to carry pollen from plant to plant."

"If Joe doesn't get here pretty soon," said the chief, "we're going to be in even bigger trouble."

"Dr. Smythe-Jones," said Cousin Fred, "how come the ant army keeps getting bigger?"

"I'm afraid it means they're creating new colonies even as they destroy Ben's farm. If that crop duster fellow doesn't get here soon, I'm afraid it'll be too—"

"I see him! I see him!" cried Babs. And

sure enough, there was Joe flying old Jenny to the rescue.

"Crop Duster Joe calling the chopper. Crop Duster Joe calling the chopper." This was Joe's first look at the super-ant army. It was the scariest thing he had ever seen. There were acres and acres of ants. "Don't be nervous, Jenny. This is the mission we were made for. Crop Duster Joe calling the chopper. Crop Duster Joe calling the chopper…"

"This is the chopper. This is the chopper. Chief Bruno here. Dr. Smythe-Jones is going to take over now. Do exactly what she says. Do you read me?"

"I read you."

"This is Dr. Smythe-Jones speaking. Here are your instructions. Follow them to the letter. Do you read me?"

"I read you."

"Descend to 300 feet. *Go no lower!* About ten percent of these super-ants can fly, and we don't want them getting on your plane. Begin your run against the wind. That's important. You don't want any of this Super DDT blowing back to you. Go in at 80 miles per hour. Got that?"

"Got it."

"Now here's your final instruction. As you begin your run, I'm going to count down from ten. When I get to 'one,' open up with the Super DDT. Is that understood?"

"Understood."

Joe checked the wind, took a wide turn, went down to 300 feet, throttled down to 80 miles per hour, and began his run. "Joe to chopper—starting my run."

The chief and Dr. Smythe-Jones had watched as Joe moved into position. The whole group had unbuckled and was now crowding the front of the cabin for a better view. They waited with bated breath.

Dr. Smythe-Jones began her countdown: "Ten...nine...eight...seven...six...five... four...three...two..." But she never reached "one."

"Attack canceled! Attack canceled!" shouted Dr. Smythe-Jones. "Take her down lower, Chief! Something strange is happening down there!"

"What is it, Minerva? Why have you canceled the attack?" asked Professor Actual Factual.

ATTACK CANCELED! ATTACK CANCELED!

"Still lower," said Dr. Smythe-Jones. "Ferdy, you're a bright young fellow. Do you see anything strange going on down there?"

Ferdy studied the scene. "Well, I see a couple of things. First, the army seems to have stopped expanding, and second, it may even be shrinking a little."

"And look!" cried Sister. "It's getting kind of brown at the edges!"

"What do you suppose it means?" asked the professor.

"I have my suspicions," said Dr. Smythe-Jones. "But the only way to make sure is to go down there and find out."

"You mean land?" said the chief.

"That's right, Chief," she said. "No, not at the center! At the edge."

"What should we do about Joe?" asked the chief.

"Tell him to keep circling until we check things out at ground zero."

"Chopper to Joe. Chopper to Joe. Keep circling until further notice."

"I'm not going to get off and walk around in those nasty ants!" said Sister. "No way!"

"That won't be a problem," said the chief. "The rotor wash'll clear 'em away!"

"That's right," said Dr. Smythe-Jones. "Especially since they'll be dead."

"Dead?"

"At least the ones at the edge."

There was an eerie feeling in the cabin as the helicopter touched down at the edge of the great ant army.

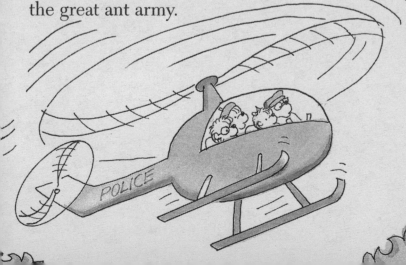

Chapter Twelve

Help for the Bens

The chief had been right. Ants flew every which way as the rotor wash cleared a big space. But there were ants as far as the eye could see. The smell of formic acid was overwhelming.

"Pee-yew!" said Sister, holding her nose. "I'm never going to drink grape juice again!"

Dr. Smythe-Jones walked over to the edge of the army. The dead ants were turning brown. She picked one up with tweezers and looked at it through a magnifying glass.

"Hmm," she said. "It's just as I suspected."

"Is it dead?" asked Brother.

"Dead as a doornail," she said.

"But look," said Babs. "Those ants in the middle are alive and kicking."

"Yes, my dear," said Dr. Smythe-Jones. "But they're kicking their last."

"What's happening?" asked Chief Bruno. "What's the explanation for all this? One minute we're looking at the worst disaster that ever struck the Earth, and the next minute we're looking at a dying army. Do you have any idea what all this is about?"

"Sorry to interrupt, Dad," said Babs. "But I think you better tell Crop Duster Joe that the crisis is over. His engine is starting to sputter."

"Good grief," cried the chief. "I forgot all about Joe. I'd better go tell him to head for home." The chief ran to the chopper and radioed Joe that the crisis had passed.

"Look over there!" said Brother. "The ants never did get to our tree house. It looks fine."

"Thank goodness for that," said Sister.

The group waved to Crop Duster Joe, who waggled his wings as he headed for his airstrip on the other side of town.

"Doctor," said the chief when he returned from the chopper, "I was asking if you had any idea what happened here."

"As a matter of fact, I think I do. But I think my good friend Professor Actual Factual does, too. I even think Ferdy might have an explanation for the strange collapse of the super-ant. Would you like to give it a try, Ferdy?"

"Happy to, Doctor," said Ferdy. He turned to the cubs. "Remember our short course in ant science back at the laboratory?"

"We remember," said Cousin Fred.

"Well, the main thing to remember," continued Ferdy, "is that *Antus maximus* was a hybrid. And you can't always predict how hybrids are going to turn out. One of the things that's hard to predict is how fast they'll reproduce. Well, as we saw, *Antus maximus* produced many, many colonies in an amazingly short time. But as sometimes happens with hybrids, they just sort of ran out of reproductive power."

"Very good, Ferdy," said Dr. Smythe-Jones. "Very good indeed! I think that's very likely what happened. But there could be another explanation. Hybrids catch certain diseases more easily than 'natural' crea-

tures. Of course, we won't know for sure until I look at some of these specimens under a microscope back at the university."

"Well, it's been quite an adventure," said the chief. "Let's head back to the helicopter and call it a day."

"Oh, dear," said Sister, looking back at the ruins of Ben's farm as they rose. "What's going to happen to our friends Farmer and Mrs. Ben? They've worked all their lives to build their beautiful farm. Now it's ruined."

"Maybe they've got some kind of insurance," said Brother.

"That would be very nice," said Dr. Smythe-Jones. "Unfortunately, I don't think you can buy insurance against the likes of *Antus maximus*. But I'm thinking about Farmer and Mrs. Ben, too. And I think the farm department back at the university may be able to help."

And that's what happened. Dr. Smythe-Jones explained the situation to the farm scientists at the university, and they arranged for Ben's farm to become an experimental farm. They had the ants

plowed under and added chemicals to thin out the formic acid. The results were excellent. Ben had fine stands of corn, wheat, and barley that year. As for his livestock, they had escaped into the neighboring forest, and they all came home wagging their tails behind them. And while Ben never got to like corn borers, wheat worms, and barley moths, he didn't mind them nearly as much as he had before.

A week or so after the great ant attack, the Bear family was sitting around in the tree house living room relaxing when a little spider let itself down on a strand of silk right in front of Sister's face. She hardly jumped at all.

Stan and Jan Berenstain began writing and illustrating books for children in the early 1960s, when their two young sons were beginning to read. That marked the start of the best-selling Berenstain Bears series. Now, with more than one hundred books in print, videos, television shows, and even Berenstain Bears attractions at major amusement parks, it's hard to tell where the Bears end and the Berenstains begin!

Stan and Jan make their home in Bucks County, Pennsylvania, near their sons—Leo, a writer, and Michael, an illustrator—who are helping them with Big Chapter Books stories and pictures. They plan on writing and illustrating many more books for children, especially for their four grandchildren, who keep them well in touch with the kids of today.